E
KRO

Kroll, Virginia L.

Hands!

300749

DATE			

HANDS!

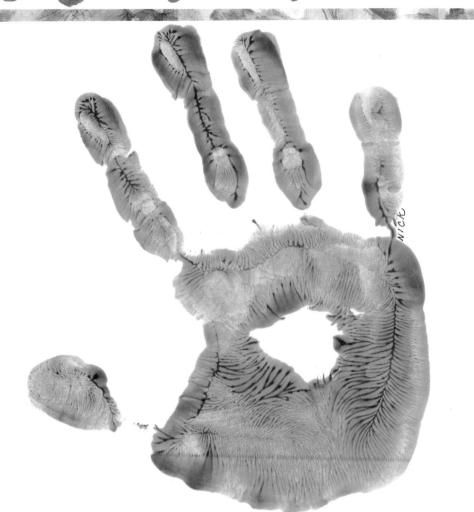

Handprints by Joseph Condren, age

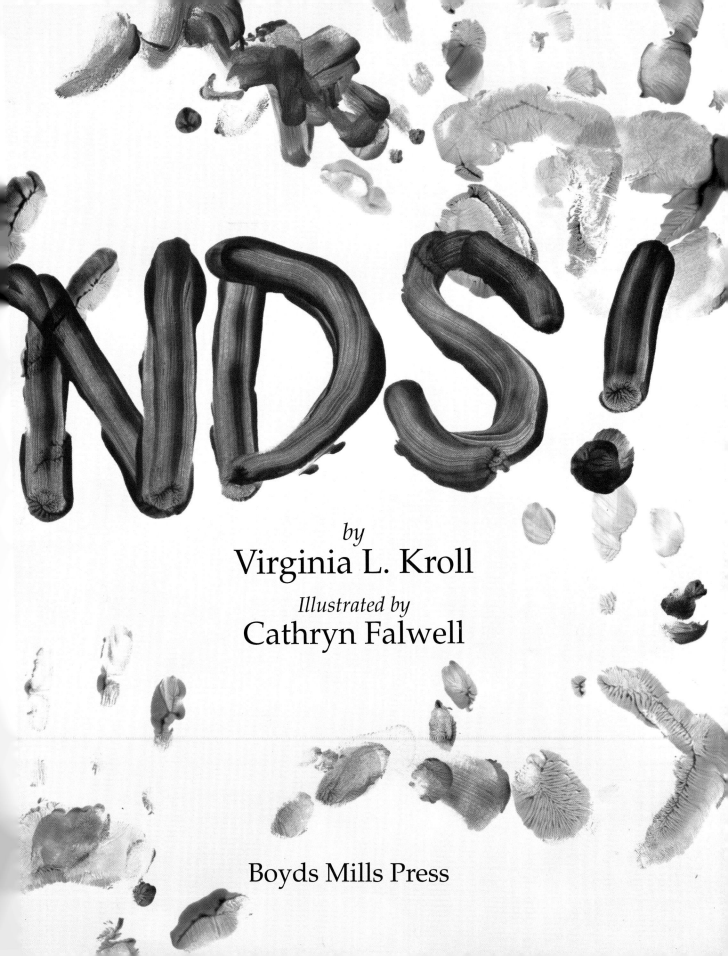

NDS!

by
Virginia L. Kroll

Illustrated by
Cathryn Falwell

Boyds Mills Press

Published by Bell Books
Boyds Mills Press, Inc.
A Highlights Company
815 Church Street
Honesdale, Pennsylvania 18431
Printed in Mexico

Publisher Cataloging-in-Publication Data
Kroll, Virginia L..
    Hands / by Virginia L. Kroll ; illustrations by Cathryn Falwell.—1st ed.
[32]p. : col.ill. ; cm.
Summary : A concept book about the many ways we use our hands.
ISBN 1-56397-051-1
1. Hand—Juvenile literature. [1. Hand.] I. Falwell, Cathryn, ill. II. Title.
612 [E]—dc20   1997   AC CIP
Library of Congress Catalog Card Number 94-72627

First edition, 1997
Book designed by Cathryn Falwell
The text of this book is set in 16-point Palatino.
The illustrations are done in cut paper and tempera.

10 9 8 7 6 5 4 3 2

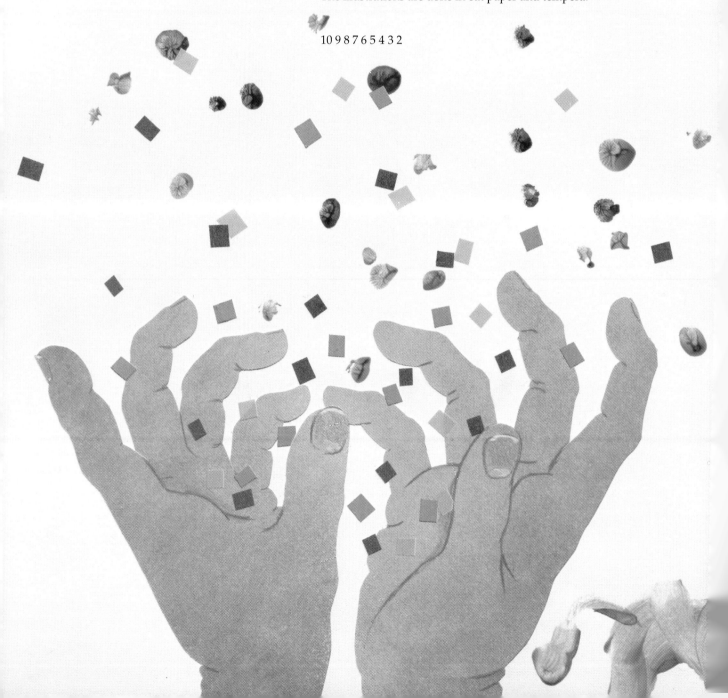

For my baby brother Christophe, with love
—V. L. K.

For Ainsley, Wylie, Gelseigh
—K. F.

Child hands
fit into
parent hands
like
perfect
puzzle
pieces.

Loving hands
join with
promising hands
to link
their lives
together.

Playful hands
cover
eager eyes
for
playing
peekaboo.

Giving hands
bring
bunches
of lilacs
to a
favorite
teacher.

Clapping hands
keep the beat
for chanting
snappy
rapping
rhymes.

Winning hands
shake
losing hands
to show
that they are
all
good sports.

Creative hands
squiggle
through
finger paints
and leave
pretty prints
behind.

Trick-or-treating
hands
scoop out
pumpkins
to turn them
into
jack-o'-lanterns.

Praying hands
clasp together
in thanks
for many
blessings.

Caring hands
cradle
colorful crayons
to write
warm
winter holiday
wishes.

Musical hands make merriment and memories.

Festive hands
throw
confetti
at
joyful
celebrations.

Black hands
fit into
white hands
into
brown hands
into
bronze hands
into
tan hands
into
beige hands . . .

. . . in a
steady
flow of
friendship.

HANDS!